52 MEN

52 MEN

LOUISE WAREHAM LEONARD

Red Hen Press | *Pasadena, CA*

Book design and layout by Mark E. Cull
Cover design by Michelle Olaya-Màrques and Marcia Langren
Cover and title page art: *Männer* by Isabelle Jelonek, Berlin
Author photo credit: Teri Fisk
Back cover photo credit: Martin Hunter, Copyright © Fairfax NZ

All other photographs from the private collection of Louise Wareham Leonard

Library of Congress Cataloging-in-Publication Data
Leonard, Louise Wareham.
  52 men / Louise Wareham Leonard.—First edition.
    pages ; cm
  ISBN 978-1-59709-996-7 (pbk. : alk. paper)
  I. Title. II. Title: Fifty two men.
  PS3623.A738A615 2015
  813'.6—dc23
                    2015006422

The National Endowment for the Arts, the Los Angeles County Arts Commission, the Los Angeles Department of Cultural Affairs, the Dwight Stuart Youth Fund, the Pasadena Arts & Culture Commission and the City of Pasadena Cultural Affairs Division, Sony Pictures Entertainment, and the Ahmanson Foundation partially support Red Hen Press.

First Edition
Published by Red Hen Press
www.redhen.org

Acknowledgments

With thanks to a few who helped me along the way:

In the U.S.—Stacey Jaffe, Alexis Hurley, Johanna Ingalls, Oliver Chubb, Allen Peacock, Bill Black and Betsy Schade.

In New Zealand, Guy Somerset; in London, Jamie Coleman.

In Germany, Isabelle Jelonek for her beautiful design work.

And to the team at Red Hen Press, especially Kate Gale, Mark E. Cull, and the Trager sisters: thank you.

To Matthew, who reminded me to write the way I want to

CONTENTS

52 MEN

What are you going to do about your loneliness?

—E.

This is a work of memory and imagination; stories, actions, and events have been changed to protect the living.

If it amounts to anything, besides a depiction of one person's life, it is a testament to the following sentiment found in an old journal of mine:

People think that life is to not get hurt.
But life is to be radical.

Part One

I

Mike was in the Navy, though I cannot see the sea in him. I cannot see ocean. We walk in the local park. It is autumn and cold and the leaves are rust colored, spiky. Mike is good looking with black hair and blue eyes. He is gentle and very quiet. When he calls me, a week later, I have a hard time placing him. "*Mike*," he keeps saying, "*Mike, Mike* from the *park*."

He works for a small college, the manager of catering. At his home, he makes me chicken parmigiana. He makes spaghetti with meatballs. He and his girlfriend went to Skidmore. Their diplomas are in matching stands, beside each other on a display case. I wonder where his girlfriend is.

He comes to my parents' house. We go out in a small steel rowboat. Mike fishes with a fishing rod we have found in a shed. Accidentally, he drops this fishing rod over the side. It sinks and though it sinks slowly, he does not dive in to get it. He stares at it and I stare at it and the metal of its handle glints as it sinks. "Please," he asks, "do not tell your parents."

2

It is sunny, and the leaves in the trees are yellowish with light and we are smoking clove cigarettes. John is tall and in sunglasses and I cannot see his eyes. I brush my toes against the grass in my red open toe shoes. When he takes off his sunglasses his eyes are blue. His hair is thick and almost white, the hair of a tennis player. He is a tennis player; he is almost a pro. He doesn't have to be though, because his family has money. He has a cottage on his father's estate. "You can stay," John says, "as long as you need to." He buys me a dress to wear to his high school reunion. He is twenty-eight and it is his tenth reunion and the dress is a cocktail dress: short and black with large multi-colored polka dots. I am not, I think, a cocktail dress girl. I wear it for him, though, and he is happy. He asks me to say I am his girlfriend.

3

Fazal is in junior high. He never likes me much, not enough to make a difference. He never kisses my face or touches my hair. His mother is a mystery: a dark eyed dark haired woman who lives somewhere else, in Saudia Arabia, perhaps, or the United Emirates. His father has a restaurant that makes hot puffy bread. It is difficult for me to be with Fazal, in the presence of his beauty. It is difficult to keep my hands from him, to keep a space between us.

Years later, I meet him at a photography reception. He lives partly in Zurich and partly in Kenya and partly in Manhattan. His photographs are of dark eyed women, of refugees and the displaced. Now that I am grown, I think Fazal might finally ask me out. Is it his fault his eyes are as shiny as melted chocolate? Is it his fault his skin is bronze in winter? He only looks at me, smiling in the warm distant way he has, as if he knows how I feel, he recognizes it, but recognizes also that it is not his responsibility.

4

Richard is a student at the School of Visual Arts. I pass him one day, on my way from the subway station, across 23rd Street toward the East River. He has long curly hair, wild rambunctious Zeppelin hair. "Can I walk with you?" he asks, standing up from his perch against the school wall. "I mean," he says, shaking out his hair, "You're so beautiful." Later, he picks me up at school on his motorcycle. I have eaten nothing that day but a packet of green Chiclets. Richard offers me a drag on his cigarette. It is a Marlboro and too strong for me. When I get off the bike, I throw up in the gutter. I leave a tiny puddle of bright green water, the green of children's toys and plastic balls. We go to Brooklyn and his windows are open. Wind blows over the bed. He kisses me. He kisses my breasts and licks my pussy. When I won't have sex with him, he tries to change my mind. What is the difference, he wants to know, between him touching me with his fingers, him licking me with his tongue—and him entering me with his cock? "There is a big difference," I say. "Not really," he says. He argues and argues with me. He argues so much that I think maybe he is a little stupid: a dead head, maybe, or a metal head. Or, maybe, he just thinks I am stupid.

5

I love Trey. As a friend I love Trey, the way friends love friends. *"Please,"* he says, *"Please,"* trying to kiss me. It isn't rape exactly. It isn't consensual either. I give in, in the end. I give in because I love him. Because I can't stand the sound of his pained voice. His want and his hankering. He keeps my earrings beside his bed. They are nice mother of pearl earrings. I would like them back but he never gives them back. He loves me. He wants to keep my earrings. For many years I will wonder where my earrings are.

6

Thor breaks my heart. He breaks it and breaks it some more. "You broke my heart," he says, "so I broke yours." He is in reform school. Then he joins the Marines. He becomes a Corrections Officer, downtown at the Tombs.

The last time I see him, I am twenty-six. We are in Central Park. It is May and the trees are full of flowers. If only, I think, things could work out. If only, for once. "Who is the one," he asks, "who has loved you since you were fourteen?" Then he shows me his gun, small and silver and strapped to his shin.

7

Klaus is German. We kiss before school, in the subway station. We kiss between cars. He tastes of cigarettes, and also oranges. We kiss in diners and record shops. Later, when I break up with him, for Billy I think, or another, Klaus cuts out the eyes in a photo of me, and mails the photo to me. He goes out with Patricia, who is beautiful. When I pass by them, standing at the benches outside school, I do not look at them. They are like trees to me, or statues of people who hold no interest. Generals, for example, or former mayors.

8

Ashley is a naïf. He is a "Just Say No" kid in the '80s. He goes to rehab at age fourteen. A year later, he is a poster boy for recovery. He is in the White House with Nancy Reagan, alone with her in a room. He can't believe they would leave him, a fifteen-year-old with a drug history, alone with the President's wife. It occurs to him that he could pick up an ashtray and bash it against Nancy Reagan's head. He doesn't, of course. But what I like is that it crosses his mind, that no matter how pretty and upright he looks, he still has a mind that makes him think of violence.

In the subway, we are inside the train. I am wearing the pendant he has given me, an eternal circle from Tiffany's. The doors open and I am about to get off, and he pulls me toward him, he clasps his hands around my back. He holds me and kisses me until the last possible second, until he lets go and I let go, and the doors whoosh closed right between us, so we both laugh. This is how we like to part, always.

At home, in my room, I take pictures of him, with his face turned up, coming. He has sweat on his chest and temple. I wipe his skin with a damp cloth. We dress and walk up to his place where he lives with his mother. He has a sleigh bed and a pennant from Dartmouth. He is twenty-eight and "the Jesus age," he laughs, meaning it is time for him to make a move.

. . .

At St. Thomas Church, on Fifth Avenue, he buys me a rose cross. The rose is for silence, the cross is for salvation. He wants to go to theological school. I run my hand through his shock of thick sandy hair. I want to marry him.

I spend a week's salary buying him a cashmere sweater. I buy him *The Oxford Book of Prayer.* We go to Central Park, up by the Castle and fields. It is autumn and cool and we sit on the damp grass. We read *The Oxford Book of Prayer.* He reads me Langston Hughes: "Feet o' Jesus." He loves this poem, he sort of sings it—*At the feet of Jesus, / sorrow like the sea. / Lordy let your Mercy* . . . He laughs. He loves Langston's Jesus with his little-boy hands.

His dream is to have a house in the Hamptons. His friends in school had houses in the Hamptons. He knows it's not that great, but a house in the Hamptons, of his own, that is his dream. Maybe, he should get an MBA. He doesn't know. He needs some sign. He feels he would be a good husband for an heiress. He goes to Outward Bound, for two weeks in the Mojave Desert. When he gets back, he meets an heiress. He marries her. Her name is Hallie and they have two sons.

Sweetness, the ground is as hard and cold here as it is anywhere on earth. I wait and wait to find something—but nothing is here. I haven't found a damn thing. When I read your letter saying "best friend" I was so honored; it moved me almost to tears. Finally, last night, the most beautiful sunset I have ever seen. It seemed as if I was being told that my faith is well placed. As is my faith in you.

9

I live with Serge, on 109th and Amsterdam. We have a dog. We have a Bonnard poster. We fight so hard we smash our pot-plants; we break a window, plates, some fingers. He wants to marry me and, "Of course," I say, when he presents a ring. "But first," I say, hesitating, turning over the ring in my fingers, "don't we need to stop fighting?"

He doesn't want to stop fighting. Fighting is "honest," he says, "and passionate," and "Italian." *Don't be too hard on me*, he writes, when I leave him with his bloody fingers, when I leave with mine. *I have loved no one as much as you. This scared me and mistakes were made.* He goes back to an old girlfriend, who is Italian, and he marries her.

10

Michael is a rock star. I don't know this at first. I think he is a guy in Mississippi, coming out of the bathroom, doing up his fly. He puts me on the guest list. On stage, he is all lit up, like Jesus on a prayer card. "Don't eat meat," he calls. "Don't quit school." Outside his hotel, all these kids want to take photographs with him. He doesn't want to take photos with them—you can tell. Still, he does. In his hotel room, with his entourage, he lies back on the bed and scratches his crotch. I think this is a little rude, though I don't say anything. I am on my way to Florida, or maybe Iowa. At the door to his tour bus, Michael tells me, "Come to Athens."

The Greyhound bus stops in Athens next to the Java Café. Michael's house is down the road, rundown and plain. His entourage is on the lawn, planting a tree. Inside, Michael is drinking blue tea. On the wall he has tacked up a long curly lock of his hair. "You know," Michael says, "I think you stopped at the Java Café. And I think you're a little nervous to be here." I am nervous. "And the thing is," he tells me, "you remind me of everything I hate about women." My chest freezes when he says this. All the air in it stands still. This remark of his—it has nothing to do with me. Later, we go out for a beer. That night, I sleep on his living room floor. The next day, I move to an abandoned house. There is no light. Cold pours through the smashed glass windows. They say he goes looking for me, but I don't hear him. I am not this bohemian, I think, and leave the next day.

II

Mr Richard Senior
539 Moortown Ring Road
Leeds 17
West Yorkshire
ENGLAND

9 November 1992

Dear Elise,

How are you doing? I was the guy you gave a cigarette to on Greenwich Avenue, Greenwich, Connecticut on a rainy day this summer. Thanks! I was having a bad day until I met you. You gave me your address and I said I might pop by one day on my travels. I never made it as I went down to Florida for some sunshine!!

I came to America on the Camp America programme and worked at a children's summer camp. It was a weird experience as I ended up getting knifed by a prick called Gerry. Anyway that was in the past and now I'm going to look forward to the future. I am going back to America on the 7th of December to take part in a court case to get some compensation for my scar—YAWN!! While I'm over there I would love to meet you again as we had a good old gossip and seemed to me to click.

My name is Richard Senior (Rich to my friends) and I'm a Politics student at the University of Teeside in Midddlebrough, England. My ambition is to be a journalist and do an M.A. at New York University. I love tennis, going out and <u>beautiful women</u>. I am 6 ft 2 in slim—not bad looking—21yrs old and am hopelessly devoted to you!

I know I hardly know you but I feel we could be great friends. Lots and lots of love

Rich xxxx
xxx
xx
x

12

Joe is in college, at River House. His ceiling is draped in silk. His walls are hung with Tibetan flags. He makes me tea. He plays me The Feelies. When it snows, he sits at the window. He smokes a cigarette so the gray smoke mixes with white. I love his quiet and his aloofness and his calm. He cares, he tells me, but not as much as most. It is something he has realized about himself. He doesn't want a girlfriend. If he has a girl, she has to fall into his lap. I fall into his lap. I love doing normal things, the way normal college kids do: drinking at the West End, eating eggs at the diner at 3:00 a.m., sitting in a seat near Joe in Introduction to Psych. Everything he takes for granted—every thing—that is the exact thing that I want.

13

Robbie has a girlfriend. I don't know about his girlfriend, or not at first. I fly from New York to London to see Robbie. I will stay in his apartment. It is an expensive apartment, a young banker's apartment because he is a young banker in Holland Park. First though, Robbie picks me up at the airport. He greets me at the gate. He places a hand on my back. He is friends with my father. They belong to a men's club, where they play squash. Robbie's hand is a comforting hand. It is a warm neat square block of a hand. I am excited at what will happen between us, at intimations that something will happen. He has plain blue eyes like flowers. He has thick sandy hair cropped close. There is nothing wily about him. There is nothing sinister or suspicious. The only suspicious thing is that he looks so unsuspicious, so content and benign, so pleasing and so good.

At the car, at the airport, it is night. He does not open the front door. He opens the back door, and when I step inside, when I sit down in the back seat, I see why he has not opened the front door. He has not done so because there is a young woman in the front seat, a rather beautiful woman. She is, Robbie says, his girlfriend.

Why has Robbie not told me about this girlfriend? Perhaps he has not told me because there is, at this point, nothing romantic between us, because declarations have not been made. It would have been, perhaps, in his mind, presumptuous of him to have told me of this girlfriend. It would have, perhaps, implied that I needed to know of this girlfriend because I myself had intentions. He did not want to imply that I had intentions. Though of course, I do have intentions, and I hope he has intentions also.

. . .

He has, as I said, an expensive apartment. It is an apartment decorated not by him, but for him. Everything in this apartment is new and neutral. The clean wine glasses are stacked face down in the glassed cabinets. Robbie, when he places his hand on my back, when he opens his (rear) car door for me, has a certain and obvious and underlying trill. Robbie vibrates, ever so gently, the way the small green throat of a bird vibrates. Robbie has desire. Robbie's desire whispers in the air.

What kind of relationship he and his girlfriend have, I do not know. She is thirty and a model for Guerlain and wants to be married. He is not sure that he is the man for this. They had broken up. They are tenuously reunited. He sets me in the guest room. It isn't where I want to be, at all. It is colder and unused. I unpack my clothes, diligently. I set out my books and toiletries. Will she stay the night, this creamy blonde non-girlfriend of Robbie's? When she watches me, it is the way an owl watches. As if her eyelids have been stretched and pinned back. She does not stay. Later, when Robbie comes into my room, I feel both happy and sorry. She is not, after all, my girlfriend. What matters to me is not how she feels—or even how I feel. What matters is how Robbie feels.

14

With Peter I am fifteen. I am in his room. It is a dark room with high ceilings. It is on 91st Street and Riverside. Rarely have I been to this side of town. Rarely have I been alone with a boy in his room. He is eighteen and a senior. Soon he is going to Tufts. He invites me to the prom. I wear a pale blue dress. It is silky, almost silvery, like water. It has a skirt, and a top with soft, scalloped straps. He is so good looking. He is olive skinned and brown eyed, quiet and gentle and almost grave. I am so afraid of this, of his goodness and his gentleness and his gravity, I find it hard to speak to him, or even look at him. We go together to *The Shining*. We go to the Dalton prom. I am too nervous to go with him to the after-party, to Danceteria where everyone goes. Because of this, most likely, Peter thinks I do not like him. I will regret this for the rest of my life.

15

Judson is a blind date. Should I dress up or down? Should I go conservative or a little indie? I have no idea what he would like. In the end, I play it in the middle: white blouse with a circular neckline, black skirt to the knees, flat shoes. What the clothes lack I can make up for with personality. He arrives in crumpled khakis and a ripped sweater. He is rich, I have been told. Yet he is also against the rich. He wants nothing to do with the world he is from. We go to an expensive restaurant in Soho. I am boring, he thinks. Where I work is boring. I want to tell him that before this, I travelled the world. I had an affair with a married man, and spent four months in a psychiatric hospital with Vitus Gerulaitis. But I am boring. I can't even choose my own clothes. When Judson hears my step-brother is a writer, he says, "Well that's interesting. Let's go see him." We sit in silence then. I feel kind of sick. "What's he written?" Judson finally asks. Then he goes slightly mad, the way I hoped he wouldn't. "*Leafscar*? No kidding. That's your brother? Wow," he says, "Wow. At least you have that."

Judson himself was going to join Greenpeace, he says, but then realized, "Why work for Greenpeace making a pittance, when I can make a whole lot of money and give it to Greenpeace?" That's why he is getting an MBA. I don't believe he will give his money to Greenpeace. I believe he is fooling himself.

"Tell your brother to call me," he says, slamming the door of my cab. I feel so bad; it is as if I've been stabbed. Twenty years later, I see him pictured in a tuxedo at the Annual Palm Beach Dinner Dance. I see him at the Frick Autumn Ball. He runs an investment fund for the assets of his family.

16

I meet Oli in the Virgin Islands. I am on assignment. He is second in command of the British Navy Destroyer the *HMS Cardiffe*. I go onboard, at dusk, to a party. Oli is in a white shirt, and a cap. He has a jacket, with stripes that gleam. He gives us a tour of the ship, and of the bridge. He is from Hampshire, he says. He is twenty-five to my twenty-eight. Later, we go to dinner. We undress by the swimming pool. He is respectful and does not look at my body. We dive naked into the still water. It is warm and smooth. The moon shines silver on his skin. His blonde hair is dark with water. Last year, he was in the Gulf War. "It was like a mallet," he says, "crushing a flea." I tell him the secret of my childhood. "So," he says, "you've had your own war."

The next day is his birthday. He asks the captain if he can call me ship-to-shore. It is his birthday, so the captain allows it. I answer the phone and hear, "This is the *HMS Cardiffe* calling Elise McKnight." Then Oli gets on the line. Oli takes a run-about to shore, then a taxi to my suite on the beach. We lie on the bed and kiss. We exchange cards. We exchange shirts and take photographs of each other wearing these. Outside, it is bright white afternoon. Massive gray rocks create a private ocean green swimming pool. In the water, out to sea, Oli lifts me up, the way a groom does, so we laugh. We are embarrassed but we can't help it. We kiss each other. We are stunned by our good luck. The water is dark green and salty and rushes in solid sweeping walls against us. Never will I be as happy.

17

Sergio* comes from school. He is seventeen and beautiful and from Queens, and before that Argentina. He has milky skin and dark eyes. He plays basketball and soccer. Later, he goes into construction. He opens a restaurant in New York City. He dates a starlet who is named for an exotic flower in Sri Lanka. In my room, we cut cocaine into sugary lines. We stay up until 5:00 am. I open the window and sit on the ledge. A breeze comes in. He straddles my desk chair, backwards. He laughs and because he laughs, and because everything is easy for him, and good, and good news—because of all this—together in the early morning, a May breeze filling my room—we write a list of all the ways to say "sexual intercourse" in the English language: *Nail. Hammer. Screw.*

*See Appendix

18

E is sorry. E is married. E should have known better. He writes from the Princeton Club and the Century Association and the Union Club. He writes year after year, when I am nineteen and twenty and twenty-nine. He cannot live without me. He cannot leave his wife. "You will marry me, won't you," he asks, "if I leave my wife?" His marriage is unbreakable. He tries to break it one night, but he goes back. He is haunted by his Puritan ancestors. He is haunted by the faces of his children. "Never," E says, "will I leave my marriage. I am a dangerous man. I have nothing but harm for you." He is my great love. I am his, this is evident. But his marriage is unbreakable. It is more unbreakable than the marriages of kings. Or princes at least, and princesses, such as Prince Charles, for example, and Lady Diana. "What are you going to do," E asks, visiting, reminding me that he cannot leave his wife, "about your loneliness?"

19

Jay is an intern at the Magazine—as am I. He goes to Yale and studies Russian and carries a gray canvas bag, one of the $5 ones from Canal Jeans. In the hallway, he leans in with his bag swinging at his thighs. He is handsome and has met my parents and loves my writing. He has thick blonde hair and blue eyes. "You are wonderful," Jay says. "Everyone loves you." He tries to kiss me but I will not let him. He is my age, we are both interns, we both go to decent schools. "It is too appropriate," I tell him, laughing, pushing him back. "What does that mean?" Jay asks, trying again, taking my hand in his. "Well, you see," I have to tell him—looking down the hall—"I am in love with an older man." "With what older man?" Jay asks and looks suspicious. I won't tell him though. I won't tell him anything. When my affair is finally discovered, it is a scandal, and worse. I lose my job and my apartment and don't know where to live.

. . .

I visit Jay at his first job in Miami. He has an "efficiency apartment" with orange shag carpet. He serves brie that is rubbery at the edges. He is unhappy there and unhappy at his job. We go to a Cuban restaurant and he is unhappy with the chicken and also the plantains. "You are so different," he says. "You are troubled and obviously on medication, and at first I hardly recognized you." We go to the Laundromat where he has a snow cone and reads Isherwood. At his apartment at night there are two single beds beside each other. He sits on one and I sit on the other. In a few years, he will marry a television news anchor. I know her—she is my age and went to my school. He will be press secretary to a President. Now, he leans back with a pillow against his lap. He cares for me, he says. He will always care. "But you're completely different," he says. Then he adds, "I can't help you." Listening to this, gripping on to my own pillow, I understand, I know he can't help. I just wish he hadn't said so.

20

We are all drunk, in this town. Roy is drunk. Barry is drunk. Jimmy Dee and sometimes Marc are drunk. Willie is drunk, when he picks me up in his crimson Chevrolet. He drives me around the delta, past the lake and cotton fields. He drives me to shantytowns and to Sledge: home of the country singer Charley Pride. "Poor Mississippi, poor Mississippi" is Willie's favorite line. We drink at the Gin. We drink at the Tavern. He gets me an appointment with William Faulkner's chiropractor. Faulkner's chiropractor tells me he knew "Will" and his brother Steve. They were both drunks. "But Will didn't write those books. Will had the ideas and Steve wrote them down." I don't believe this. Willie doesn't believe it either. Barry calls me, drunk, and asks if I will be Willie's wife.

21

In Central Park, the reservoir is inky. There is no moon. The only light is from the clouds: from all the traffic lights red yellow and green inside them, all the tail-lights and head lights and street lamps pooled into rose pink. Adam* pulls me under a tree. It is an oak tree and full of leaves. "Don't you like me?" Adam asks. "Because I like you," he tells me, "*a lot.*" I am not sure I want him to like me *a lot.* When he kisses me, against the leaves, it is as if he is hungry.

He wears his keys on a silver chain attached to his belt. He wears denim jeans and a cropped denim jacket. He is a scholarship student from the Bronx and at the school dance, we dance so hard to the Buzzcocks, it is like we electrocute ourselves. "You didn't like me before tonight, did you?" I ask, lying back on the leaves.

"Of course I did."

"You never thought about me before, did you?" I ask.

. . .

"Of course I thought about you, I thought about you lots of times." He rests on his elbow. "Haven't you thought about me?"

I feel bad then. I stare at the pink sky. "Actually," I say slowly, "I kind of have a boyfriend." Adam looks disappointed. "Oh really?" he asks, his face in half shadow, his voice sounding so sad it is worse and worse. Then he cheers up. He fingers the collar of my blue shirt, my favorite one, with tiny red flowers. "Can't you tell him you've met someone else?" I am very quiet. "I don't think so," I say. "Do you want me to tell him?" he asks. It scares me how much he likes me. "Or, I can wait," he says. He is so kind. I escape his kisses, I escape his grasp. I run home down Park Avenue like a sprinter on a track field. His liking will catch me up. It will swallow me. I will never be free.

*Adam Lewis, dies 9/11, World Trade Center, age thirty-six

22

Charlie "Love" Jacobs* is from Jackson, Mississippi. He plays saxophone and harmonica with his band at the Gin. His face is white as a boy drowned in a lake. His eyes are pale blue and he comes over after his gig. I am upset when I hear he lives with a girlfriend in Jackson. "You didn't know that?" he asks. "No," I say, "I didn't." "Then what do you know?" "I heard you shot up drugs, with your ex, to make yourselves climax." "That's true," Charlie says. "But she's not my ex. Do you want me to do that with you?" "Not really," I say. We try to have sex and I want to have sex. Instead, I start to cry. At twenty-three, it has been two years since I have let a man touch me. "I can't touch you," he says, "if you cry." "Why can't you?" "You're hurt, you're too hurt," he says and turns away from me in the bed. Ten years later he dies of "the Life" at thirty-nine. He is buried in Clark Mound Cemetery in Beulah in the Delta.

*Charles Jacobs III, dies 4/1997, age thirty-nine

23

Greg is in Key West. He comes busting through the screen door, one Saturday night, in June. He is tall and tanned from the sun, his face ravaged and his eyes fire blue, opals. In my hand he places a rose, plucked from a roadside bush. Not even on a bed, but on some pallet on the floor, we lie all night, hardly sleeping, damp from the heat and each other's bodies. We are between sleep, between waking, lust and desire all through us, a kind of urgency as if it is our last chance. It is our last chance. In the morning, at 6:00 a.m., he takes me to my scheduled flight. In the terminal, we are breathless, dizzy. Our hands lock together; his lips return to my neck, cheek, temple. My lips return to his. He gives me a card for my wallet with three words on it: *Expect a Miracle*. It takes a long time to realize that this is it, this is how a miracle feels.

24

Billy's eyes are all pupil. Billy's eyes are metal ore. This is from the drugs. From the cocaine like the whites of his eyes, in shiny clear plastic packets, slivered and sliced up ice, baby powder with a slick of glass. He gives it to me after school, in his room. His favorite drink is 7&7 and he gives me several of these, too. Billy has another girlfriend. Her name is the name of a ballet. My parents take me to the ballet and in the first act the girl is alive and in the second act she is dancing on her grave. I see Billy's girlfriend one day at school. She doesn't go to our school. She goes to another school, across town. She is visiting this day. I feel sick and faint and cannot breathe. She is small and dark and looks nothing like me.

Billy does not want to do that thing to me, to do that thing called two-timing. "You are too good for that," he says. "I would never do that to you." Still, he does do it. He does it and does it again. Later, he goes to art school. He moves to Colombia. He becomes a stockbroker and his Facebook page says he is in an open relationship with a woman named Marta.

25

I call Steven from a phone booth on 91st Street and Lexington. He is thirty-four and a bartender and going back to school. It is night and a man comes up behind me and presses either the barrel of a gun or something meant to feel like the barrel of a gun into my back. "Your wallet," he says. "Your watch. Your rings." Talking to this man, calming him, at the very least trying to acquiesce to him, I am overheard by Steven, whose voice on the phone goes shrill with fright—the way a girl's must, realizing she won't get away. Later, he runs me a bath. He lights a vanilla candle. He pours me red wine. All night we lie together, his embrace like floating, like being high, like poppies. "I wouldn't work where you work," he says. He would only work at *National Geographic*.

26

I meet John in a meadow. His art is everywhere—1,000 pound steel balls, five foot in diameter—strewn across the grass. A month later, he is outside St. Vincent's Hospital. He has just been inside, he says, for three weeks, for depression. His eyes are saucers: round and wet and navy blue like kids' watercolors in white plastic trays. "*Elise*," he says, "*Elise*," and steps right inside me. "Have you ever been depressed?" "I have," I say and think maybe I can help him.

In two months, we get engaged. He is older: forty-two to my twenty-seven. This means nothing to me, except for the wives. The third calls me up. *Oh Honey*, she writes on my windshield. Then she smashes the windshield.

His first never would give him a divorce, so officially he is a bigamist with his second. The second is a performance artist, John says, and sends performance videos. In them she dances naked in a giant barn, stopping occasionally to talk to the camera. "That's not performance art," I say, "that's her sending videos of herself naked, and talking to you." It is true, John says, from the floor where he is watching, she does talk to him in the video, but "mostly, she sings." "But she sings Suraba-ya Johnny! That's your name." He looks startled. "Johnny's a very common name." He starts to stammer. "Anyway listen to her—" he waves at her singing on the screen.

. . .

I hate you! Take that damn pipe out of your mouth you rat—

"She's calling me a rat! A rat or a swine or a bum! Every video it's a different version."

"John," I say.

"I miss her," he says, getting to his knees, groping for my thighs.

"I miss you," he says, and clutches at my waist. "I miss every-one."

I cannot take your pain, I write, in the letter that I leave him.

27

Carter* lives on the East River, in a high rise apartment. The wind blows down the river and around the building and into the city. "You're lucky," he says, "you weren't a child in this city. There are children in the city who have never seen the ocean. Can you imagine that?" he shakes his head. "*Terrible.*"

He loves the ocean. He loves where I grew up, in Montauk: a small town, by the sea, no celebrities, no phonies. Or at least not *Catcher in the Rye* phonies. At least not phonies who only talk to you because your mother is a celebrity and your family rich. He hates that. He has an older brother who hates it also; he ran away to Vermont a few years ago and no one knows where he is.

We go from his room, outside onto the terrace. It is fourteen flights up. The wind rushes around our bodies and through our hair. His eyes light up, looking out at the boats and distance. He sets down a blanket and we have a glass of wine. Night comes down like black paint. We are sixteen and there is so much he wants to do. He likes to walk around the city taking photographs of things he sees. Sometimes he goes to parties and just watches people. "It seems to me," he says, "that sometimes people—especially girls," he laughs, "have one beautiful little gesture they make, one characteristic thing."

. . .

Maybe, he says, we could take the train out to Montauk. Or we could go to Vermont and find his brother. We are not city people, are we? Whenever he thinks of me, he says, he thinks of the ocean.

Over the summer, he sends me a postcard of the ocean by Vija Selmins. He sends me a copy of *Rooms by the Sea* by Edward Hopper. For college, he goes to Princeton. He has the same girlfriend for three years. When they break up, he gets depressed. He comes home and leaves his tennis bag at the door. He goes to his room, and later out to the terrace. Everyone gets depressed. Everyone we know. But whereas I always feel too much, Carter feels nothing. This is what he tells his mother just before he drops off the terrace to his death. Actually, he asks her, "Will I ever feel again?" and none of us know, none of us will ever know.

*Carter Cooper, dies 7/1987, age twenty-three

28

Joel is from Queens and a graphic designer. He has a loft apartment in Soho. In this apartment is a swing. You can swing from the light of the windows on the east side toward the darkness on the west. Joel makes me cards: homemade carefully wrought works-of-art cards. Joel gives me a photograph of two trees leaning toward each other. He writes on a card: *You are the light at the end of the tunnel.* Not long after this, he changes his mind. "You are angry at me," he says, "You are frequently angry and I do not know why." For my thirty-second birthday, he gives me a bicycle, a red Villager cruiser. We go biking in the afternoon through the streets of New York. We bike to the Lower East Side and across the Brooklyn Bridge. He is happy with me. This happiness, however, does not last. Joel decides he no longer wants to see me. "You are too angry," he says. "You are angry for some reason I don't know. I don't cause your anger. Something does, but it is not me and I can't heal it."

29

Paul is a waiter and also an actor. He takes me home and hands me a lance. He is a jouster. He jousts with me. "I want to joust with you," he tells me, "so you always remember."

30

I meet Bob at a dinner party on Gansevoort Street. I have come late to the party so as to miss dinner. I can't afford dinner, so come for coffee. Bob notices this. Bob comments on it. Bob is impressed, he says. He is a lawyer, Insurance Coverage and Litigation. He lives on 35th Street. He has a house in Rhinebeck. He drives me there and it is spring. It is April but not summer. We lie back on his sun warmed bed. It is blue, and also quiet. He hardly touches me. This is how seriously he takes me. He tells me he is serious and he acts serious. He takes me to his parents' house in Greenwich, Connecticut. They are in their early eighties, full of plenitude. We walk by their ocean and "you have the body of a nineteen-year-old," he says, "I love that; I want to marry that." "That?" I repeat. "Yes," he smiles, "That." Something in my chest starts to rise. Something catches my lungs so they stop moving. "What if I don't always have the body of a nineteen-year-old?" I ask. "But you plan to," he says. "Don't you?" I weary, sometimes, of how easy men are—both to please and to lose. "Oh, for God's sake," I say. "Oh," Bob says, pulling back from me, groping for his car keys. I have an urge to slap him. I do not slap him, but my body wants to. As much as he is afraid of me, as much as that and more, I despise him for his fear.

31

Lou is in a hot tub, alone me with me at the Chelsea Piers, the most expensive club I belong to. It has windows on the Hudson. It has velvet light. He stands up to let the water flow over him, and I see his package. I am embarrassed by this. I know his package has been the subject of attention. He sees me looking, but I look away. Always it is this way, with the famous. Pretending not to know them when "Sad Song" fashioned all my dreams. "Oh," I say to him finally, so he squints at me, hoping I haven't spoken. "You know my brother." His eyes are the color and depth of wall painted black. "Who is your brother?" he asks.

His voice is very deep. It is the deep of the mad, of the man I always try to make love me, the one who does finally love me, until I realize his love is not worth as much as I'd thought. "Ben Galogly," I say. "Ben." His eyes light up with a fascinated horror, the way they always do for Ben, though not so much for me. "Congratulations," he says.

32

Quentin is a storyteller. By which he means, he likes to tell stories—not on paper—but out loud, to an audience. He has done this on a soap box in London. He has done it on a soap box in Prospect Park. In ten years he will be a celebrated storyteller at The Moth. A filmmaker will film his stories. Quentin will be the new Carver to the new Altman and make a zillion dollars and move to Hollywood.

When I know him, however, he is a storyteller and paints apartments. He paints apartments for money while he finesses his stories. Sometimes the paint fumes make him sick and the stories veer off or crash. Sometimes a view he catches out a window inspires flashes. "It is important," Quentin says, "to take one's storytelling to extremes." He would like, for example, to tell stories on Mt. Fuji, "or underwater where gesture is so important."

He is thirty-seven, as am I. "We are starving artists," he laughs, "surrounded by the feast. Perhaps we should starve in a place that is not so full of plenty." He is simple and good, I think, without the aspirations I usually hate. He has a neat perfect boy face: boyish skin, boyish short brown hair, boyish blue eyes. He wears gray suits and white shirts. It's cheaper that way. Also, he can launch into any character without having to change clothes.

. . .

We go to readings. We go to plays and sit in the front rows, gesticulating and occasionally laughing. We have such a good time, people tell us to be quiet. We go to see *Medea* and just when Medea kills her children on stage, a man in the audience has a heart attack. A crowd of people gather around him, calling 911 on their cell phones. "Quentin," I urge, "you should help."

Of course he'll help, but "just give me a minute," he says. It is a great story—a heart attack during *Medea*—he has to get it down in his mind. He jumps up to get some chocolate raisins from Refreshments; sugar helps him focus.

After the performance, we spot a famous editor and writer. "Fantastic," Quentin says, "he's a friend of mine."

"Oh, no," I say, "he's not really, is he?" When I was a teenager, I took the editor's workshop at Columbia. He was famous for wearing safari outfits in the city, for running six-hour workshops in which no one could use the bathroom, and most of all, for stirring up his students.

Once, for example, he asked if he could jack off to my story in the toilets. He asked me this in class, before two hundred students. I was eighteen and never spoke to him again; I tried to, but I was mute.

. . .

"That is a good story," Quentin thinks. "But look, that was years ago. He's changed." He has changed, too. "Remember Elise?" Quentin asks him. "You humiliated her. You asked her if you could jack off to her story." The editor does not remember me. I feel humiliated. I have kept my hurt feelings for almost twenty years. The editor apologizes. "Oh the scars," he smiles, "that last forever." He lifts up his shirt and shows me his scars from cancer surgery. I show him my scars from a fire when I was three. Another good story, we all laugh.

Quentin and I end up at his apartment. It is in Queens and has aqua blue aluminum siding. Everything in it looks dragged from the sidewalk. The bed has a thin fitted sheet with broken elastic, so the sheet slips and slides all over the mattress. It is night and the only light is from a lamp across the street. Quentin has an odd way of kissing without opening his mouth. He keeps his lips pressed together, so it is like kissing an old person. I don't ask him about this. If this is how he likes to kiss, it is all right with me. Then Quentin asks, gesturing to the end of the bed, "Why don't you get down on the floor," he pauses, and gestures again, "why don't you get down on all fours and move your fingers in and out of your asshole?"

I look at his face but he is not laughing. "Why don't you?" I ask. He doesn't answer that. I feel a great weariness and pull the top sheet over my face. I remember when I was a teenager and saw a man masturbating in Central Park. It was evident to me that the man when he looked at me was hoping for some kind of reaction. "Don't react to him," my mother would say, in that sort of situation. "Don't give him the satisfaction."

33

I am lying on Ron's couch. The copy of Rilke you
gave Jamie rests on the table. I think of you often.

There are other reminders, too. Your name and
number, in large, dark writing, tacked to the
Nokia wall. I've been calling for a long time. No
answer, or you are just "away from white." Finally
to where you ~~are~~ now, but still no answer.

Walking to my house in the rain, one late night.
It rains now - the first in three weeks.
Then there is an inescaple reminder, inside of me,
where you have left fingerprints.

I want to do so much. I don't even know
what you are being "treated" for. I cannot sit idly by,
and patiently watch a progression of events unfold
for you. The consequences of that are too great.
But for now I can only give this letter and offer
what I find in my own life: peace, hope and love
I want you to have these

I love you
Blaine

I am lying on Ron's couch. The copy of Rilke you gave Jamie rests on the table. I think of you often.

There are other reminders, too. Your name and number, in large, dark writing tacked to the Hoka wall. I've been calling for a long time. No answer, or you are just "away for a while." Finally to where you are now, but still no answer.

Walking to my house in the rain, one late night. It rains now—the first in three weeks. Then there is an inescapable reminder, inside of me, where you have left fingerprints.

I want to do so much. I don't even know what you are being 'treated' for. I cannot sit idly by, and patiently watch a progression of events unfold for you. The consequences of that are too great. But for now I can only give this letter and offer what I find in my own life: peace, hope and love. I want you to have these.

I love you.
Blaine.

*Blaine Pitzer, dies 3/2014, age forty-seven

34

Andreas* is in Greece. I meet him on his yacht, the 218-foot *Rosenkavalier*, built in 1929. He is one of nine children born to a shepherd. He made his fortune in donuts, and later cream-filled pastry puffs. "Come," he says, "Sail with me. I will give you your own suite. You can do your work on the aft deck."

I take a photo of him on a wicker chair, drinking champagne. The light is gold mixed with silver. His face is dark from tanning. His smile is very white. His wife is Orthodox and will not divorce him. In the morning, he sends me a large stately hardcover cloth book, *Burke's Peerage*. There is an article on him and his rise from donuts.

In the afternoon, he takes me to a boatyard. His new yacht is there, all steel lines, massive as a ferry. "You will sail on it," he says. "You will write about it." He is a small man, with a small bullish chest. He has all his hair and kind dark eyes: not dark like coal or iron ore or night. But brown like a dog's eyes—a spaniel or beagle.

. . .

He has four children. His son's name is Dionysius. I don't meet his daughters. When I get home to New York, Andreas calls me up. "I followed you," he says. "I arrive tonight, via Miami." He has his own plane.

I take him to the Village Vanguard. It could be wonderful, I think, to sail with him, to have my own suite, to work on the aft deck. He shows me the suite—he has a brochure. The bedspread is shiny black. The drapes are gold. "Or, you could have the petal room," he says. It is delicate, like tendrils, pale green and yellow. "Lalique," he says, when I touch the bowl in the photograph. "Fantasia."

At the Vanguard, it is dark and smoky. A band plays the blues and he likes the blues, he says. He understands the blues. "Do you," he asks, "understand the blues? Perhaps not yet." He lays out his business card. He adds a number to it. "Come tonight," he says, meaning to the Mediterranean. "Come next week. I will arrange it."

. . .

We don't eat. He is past eating. We drink champagne. I am twenty-seven and wearing a short skirt. I am wearing a pale peach silk shirt that is shoulderless and wrapped at the neck. The lights lower. The lights lower again. He has his right arm around my shoulder. He lowers his hand to my breast. He takes his finger and his thumb and squeezes my nipple. He crushes it. Although this hurts so much that I hold my breath, I stay very still, very quiet, I pretend not to notice. What I do notice is that he has warned me. What I do notice is that never will I sail with him in the Aegean. Never will I swim with him or write about him on his aft deck.

Later, he builds the *Alysia*. It is 280 feet. It has thirty-six crew. Weekly rental is 661,500 Euros ($820,000). He is in Mumbai at a trade show. He leaves his boat in the harbor and goes in search of a curry to eat. It is 2008 and he dines at the Palace. Islamist fundamentalists overtake the Palace. He and his fellow guests are locked in the basement. Andreas uses his cell phone to call his family and then the BBC. His last words describe a lull in the bombing. You can hear them online: "All we know is the bombs are next door and the hotel is shaking every time a bomb goes off. Everyone is just living on their nerves." He is shot five times and dies at seventy-three.

*Andreas Liveras, dies 11/2008, age seventy-three

35

Hewson realizes that he is not interesting enough, that he is in finance and needs new interests, to make him more interesting. For this reason, he takes a course in astronomy. He joins the American Museum of Natural History. He is sorry he doesn't know more about my profession—or any of the arts really—but he appreciates my bearing with him, my answering questions, our differences. He is of the age (thirty-nine) where he would like to be married and it would be nice ultimately to have someone different than himself, someone to counterbalance his own interests, bring something new to the table.

He is a worry, this Hewson, how earnest yet how unusual, with this humility about his failings. He is from a long-established family. His clothes and his face and his hair are quintessential WASP. A friend jokes that his blandness and awkward charm could actually hide a serial killer, but this is somehow so true that we barely laugh. We decide I should not visit his apartment until more is known.

Over the course of six or seven dates, he is very hard to read. He dances with me at a formal dance, but does not kiss me; he walks with me in various outdoor and indoor settings but never takes my hand. Is he interested or not interested? Maybe, I hope, he just needs more time. Then again, if he is not interested, he should back off. I am not his instructor in the arts of how to be interesting.

. . .

Then one early morning, I am leaving a party we have both attended. I have talked on this night to several men—to Hewson, to Timothy, and to Jamie who are openly interested in me. I might let Timothy or Jamie walk me home. Both offer. Still I am drawn to Hewson. I want to give him a chance. I want to move things forward. So when he asks, several times, almost aggressively over the attentions of Timothy and also Jamie, I say "*Yes*," relieved almost at his passion, "yes of course, you can walk me home."

I live almost two miles—eighteen blocks—from the party. It is very late, almost two thirty, and no woman in the city walks home alone at that hour. If a man were not walking me I would ride in a cab and when the cab arrived at my apartment building, the cab driver would wait at the curb and see that I got safely inside my front door and locked it behind me. He might even get out of his cab and walk me to my door—some do.

Hewson and I amble slowly, chatting, pulling our scarves around our throats, ten blocks, fourteen blocks, sixteen blocks toward my apartment building. It is then 3:00 a.m. I see this on the outdoor clock on 10th Street. A couple passes us in between bars. Otherwise, the streets are dark, bleak, deserted. Two blocks from my building, Hewson stops suddenly. "Well," he says, and salutes me with one hand. "Good night," he says and steps away uptown.

36

Timothy is a favorite. He lives on Prince Street and rides a Moto Guzzi motorbike and helps the poor in Bushwick. In his wallet, he keeps a poem of mine, about Jesus, and rage, but mostly rage. We go to the Odeon, and Pravda. His favorite bird is the sparrow. When I leave town, to work upstate, he gives me the *Audubon Field Guild to Northeastern Trees.*

We meet at the Candlelight, between towns, in Massachusetts. They have electric candles along the window sills. He buys me hiking boots. He washes my car and fits it for emergencies. We hike the Appalachian Trail. We sleep on mountains. We follow creeks and mushrooms. He is broad shouldered and tall. He wears shorts and thermal tops. He wears red hiking socks and a Tilley hat. I am thirty-six and would like a baby. "A *baby*," he repeats, in his apartment, as if this is a dirty word.

I never go back, except to pick up my things. I find a list of pros and cons about me. *Pro: Great sex. A good person. Con: Needy, both emotionally and financially.* In six months, he impregnates a soap actress. They marry and have two children.

37

Tom is in Hoboken. He loves Hoboken. He takes me to Leo's Grandevous. Sinatra has been there. It serves chicken parmigiana. Tom is sweet. Tom is nice. He is a photographer and sweeps me up—he snaps me the way a photograph is taken: suddenly, the shutter falling, snap. Then he carries me around, as if he has me, as if I am an image fully formed and living inside his head. Thumbelina comes to mind: that pretty elf—or fairy—who grew up in a flower.

We go to Ellis Island, for a story he is doing. We go to Milton with his friends. They have a banana boat and we ride on it, though I am embarrassed by this. Then we go to yoga camp, in Bermuda. Our room is white. It is in the shape of an igloo. It is called Igloo Room. I hate Igloo Room. I hate it and I hate yoga and I hate Tom. It has only been a few months and he is in my bed, in Bermuda, at a yoga camp. I can hardly touch him. I can hardly look at him. I stick close to the edge of the bed, as if to a hanging bed, canvas, in a boat in a great storm. Back in New York, he calls me up. "We are two very different people," he says, and breaks it off. Six months later, on 12th Street, I run into him. "What happened to us?" he asks.

38

I meet Eddie on Central Park West, in Columbus Circle at midnight. It is summer and the trees are whirling with dry leaves and it is my first year with my first apartment: I can do whatever I please. Eddie is walking a black Labrador. He walks me uptown, to my apartment, and outside, under a street lamp, I see his face in the soft light. He is nondescript. Nothing about him stands out. He is twenty-eight, he tells me, and a salesman for a telephone company. "Do you have to go inside?" he asks.

I am twenty years old. I am completely free. At the same time, I confess, I cannot get involved with him. "I am in love," I tell him, "with a married man." We walk to the park and sit on a bench. He has something good to smoke, he tells me, under the maple trees, "Would you like to try?"

That summer, all summer, we spend the weekends in his apartment by Columbus Circle. It is a one bedroom on the seventeenth floor and he has a queen mattress on a base. He has a stack of videos and books about the penal system, and *The Hitchhiker's Guide to the Galaxy*. My lover, my married man, is busy with his wife, so Eddie and I smoke all night. We pass the pipe back and forth, back and forth, between us. Sometimes the pipe burns my lips, and sometimes my lungs are too full to breathe. Eddie's Labrador doesn't like the smoke either and Eddie feels badly about this; we keep meaning to take her out. We often don't, though.

. . .

The apartment fills up with the smell of rum and smoke and we play cards, we play backgammon. Never does Eddie try to kiss me. He respects I am in love with a married man. Because he works for the phone company, he gives me the latest telephone model. It has a red light on the top, like an ambulance—the light blinks silver and red when the phone rings.

One time he takes me to Long Island to meet his mother. He asks me to wear his favorite dress: a yellow dress with straps. His mother's house is small and very neat. It has a concrete porch on the side. She serves a lemon drink because, we notice, it is still summer. "How long have you and Eddie," she asks, "been together?"

Later, when my married man leaves his wife, then goes back to her the next day, I decide to leave the country. This happens so quickly, I don't even say goodbye to Eddie. I imagine he calls and his phone keeps ringing in my apartment, me flying overseas, the little red light blinking: *Emergency, Emergency.*

39

Generous of you to write, considering the rather over-the-top nature of my letter. I wrote that in an emotionally charged state and I believe I exaggerated many things. I certainly felt a good deal of contrition immediately after sending it, and to its tone. But I never could be direct with you, and my frustrations kept building until that Sunday morning they exploded in a rather unseemly way. Generous, then, that your anger didn't keep you from eventually responding. I do not expect any "answers" from you, and not withstanding any silliness I may have put down as to rules in relationships, I agree that conditional relationships are absurd. More than requiring anything of you, I just had to express my anger. Perhaps that's lame, selfish, cowardly, or worse. I suppose these are my true faults coming to the fore. In any case, though, I guess we weren't getting along for one reason or another; I was annoying to you; you acted in ways I couldn't understand or deal with. And now I have written things that have injured you, perhaps irrevocably. So your suggestion of silence may be the best after all.

40

Tony is from Liverpool: he is a boxer, and also an actor, and of a formidable size. I hardly know him but he takes me to the Turkish Baths on East 12th Street. He throws me in the cold water, then the hot, then the ice. He thrashes me with eucalyptus fronds and massages me in the steam room. He does all this, over and over, for two hours. He takes me into a shower stall and cuts my hair, because he is also, he says, a hairdresser. He lies me in a cot and feeds me carrot juice, and later borscht. When we get outside, he veers into a bookstore and reads me Neruda: *In the dark pines the wind disentangles itself. . . .*

41

Bruce is small and boxy, and his fat mouth hangs open some-times, and is wet; when he fights with the other boys in the schoolyard at lunch, his mouth drools. He wipes it with the back of his hand, embarrassed, but not so much that he will stop fighting. He is in love with me, though I prefer Brian, who has soft white blonde hair and is himself in love with Tracey Atkinson. Bruce gives me a pen: a fat crimson Parker pen; maybe he bought it, maybe his father is a banker and the pen is from a banker's personal home collection. It comes in a Parker box, heavy, with a satisfying snap when it both opens and closes. He gives me a 14-karat gold-plated bracelet, with thick links and a bar with my name engraved on it: *Elise,* in loopy floral writing. "You cannot accept this bracelet," my parents say. "You are too young for such a bracelet." But what will Bruce do with a bracelet with *Elise* curled into it? Lunchtimes, he buys me cola ices, Glugs, in the shape of triangles. I let him kiss me, once, behind the deserted house. I feel sorry for him. I know he will never be satisfied, not by me.

42

Peter is small, he is fast, he is seven. In class one day, his friend
hands me a note. "It is a love note," the friend says, "from Peter."
Inside this note is a black smudge: crushed body of a black fly,
wings broken, round oily hot eyes.

43

Jonathan is the world's most famous North American novelist. He isn't when I meet him. He is an unknown: modest and almost shy, fundamentally but not impossibly handsome. He has come to the arts colony to read from his new book. It is a novel, coming out in a month. In the kitchen, I cut him hunks of bread and cheese. We have both just been through breakups. We are miserable and barely able to go on. We smile as we say this, but they are rueful smiles full of understanding.

After he leaves, he sends me a postcard. On it is a black and white photograph of a white sheeted bed. I don't know what this photograph suggests, or if it suggests anything. It seems, however, to suggest something.

Two months later, his new book comes out. It wins 434 awards. It sells 800 million copies. It appears in 269 languages. It seems he and his girlfriend are working something out.

He comes to my city to give a reading. We plan to go to dinner. The reading is in the Town Hall. There are 800 people there. I wait two hours by the signing table. Finally, I lead him from Town Hall through the city past the Bucket Fountain. He has been away, by the ocean. He doesn't like the ocean, though. He likes cities. "Do you like this city?" I ask. He looks around. "The best thing about this city is you."

. . .

At dinner, he has the local fish: paua. Then I take him driving. I have just bought a car—two days ago. It was $3,000 at auction, champagne colored and American. I take him on a joyride, up and down and around the roily hills, up a 650-foot-high mountain where I accidentally back into a hillside, smashing into rocks. The night is dark. The wind is fierce and vigorous. We climb up to look at the harbor lights. "Do you believe in God?" I ask. "That's a bit personal." "So, are you back with your girlfriend?" He hesitates. He is, he says. At the same time, she isn't so strict about things. Which is a relief. *I bet*, I think, taking him to see a bust of a royal.

Eventually, that night, we pull up outside his hotel. He presses his long fingers together. "It doesn't feel right," he says, "to leave you alone." Is he suggesting something? He seems to be, but I am not sure. I refuse always, at this point in my life, to sleep with a man who has another girlfriend. Still, for a moment, I think about it. I remember his novel in which a character masturbates on a couch. I hated that scene so much it is hard to imagine having sex with its author. Then again, he is somewhat handsome. "You should get out of the car," I tell him, "or I might have to kiss you."

The next day, I find out that my car is riddled with rust. It is "highly dangerous" and could "split apart" and "shatter" at any time. It must be immediately destroyed. *Imagine*, I think, *if the car had "split apart" and "shattered"* while I was driving the world's most famous North American novelist. Now I would be famous also.

44

Steve is a police officer. I watch him calming down some men in a fight in Soho. I am so impressed by this—by his calmness and his presence and quiet authority—I begin talking to him. He is forty-two and retiring next year. He has seen gruesome things, he says, mentioning a head in a bucket. Yet somehow he is unjaded. He is light and gentle and almost pure. Last year, he tells me, he "shot an individual in the line of duty." The individual didn't die, but Steve is being given a medal for bravery. Do I want to come to the awards ceremony, Steve asks? I do. It is near Police Plaza, one Saturday in August. I wear my best clothes. Steve and fifteen thousand other police wear their blue uniforms. Mayor Guiliani is there and applauds all the bravery. We receive a pamphlet about bravery and it turns out that all the acts of bravery being honored today involved the shooting of individuals.

At Steve's apartment, that night, we play with his martial arts equipment, his balancing pole and punching bag and nun-chuks. We look at photos of him scuba diving in the Caribbean. "My brother's been in prison," I say suddenly. "What, in New York?" Steve asks. "In Rikers, lots of times. For drugs." We lie on our backs on the bed and he opens his fanny pack. He takes out his gun, which he keeps in there. "Here," he says, "do you want to hold it?" I do want to. It is, I think, *aerodynamic*. It is black and heavy and blocky. I point it at my feet, at the wall, at the ceiling. When I put it down, I feel very tired. It is not, I realize, something a person like me should have.

45

I meet Henri at a wedding. He is French. He is beautiful, in a beautiful suit. He doesn't see me at first, he is not looking for someone to see. This is why I notice him. Later, we walk on the rocks, by the ocean. It is California. His hands are tan and smooth. We move up to the swimming pool. I am wearing a red bathing suit and he adjusts its strap. In the deckchair, I lie against him, my red suit against his warm flesh.

"Stay with me," he says, that night. *It is too soon*, I say. "I will not touch you," he says. *No*, I say. "I will not touch you," Henri promises. *No*, I say. "Just to be together, just to have you near me." *No, really.* This goes on for a long time, probably for one hour. Never before have I done battle with a Frenchman. *All right*, I say, finally. *But I will not have sex with you.* "Of course," Henri promises: "I will not touch you." Early the next morning, I wake up with him having sex with me. I am so angry at this, I start to cry. Then I realize: it's too late. We can't go back. We are already having sex. Also—what am I going to do? Scream and ruin the wedding? I give in, then. I join in. *Go on*, I say to myself. *Make it mean something. Make it matter.*

46

Jamie is good, he is kind, he works on Wall Street. He is tall and well-built and has short reddish hair. His grandfather was a general. His father is an ex-diplomat living in Bermuda. When his mother died, of cancer, she left Jamie her fortune. His father sued but was unsuccessful. When I go to Jamie's apartment once—I have known him for ten years—there is a photograph of me in a frame by his bed. He takes me to the Union Club. He takes me to Tuxedo Park. He gives me my own room, painted yellow with a vase of freesia. In the *en suite* are porcelain soap dishes in the shapes of clam shells. I watch Jamie play squash, and *jeu de paume*. We sit by the fire and "there is more," he says, more to know. He sends me postcards from Rome. He takes me to Christmas Mass at St. Thomas Church. "Maybe this could be a time for us?" he asks—once every year or two, offering this, and himself, to me—but I turn away, I shield myself as if I do not deserve it.

47

Charlie is a writer. I have a poem of his on my wall: "Mother at Eighty." Later, I throw out his poem. I throw out his books of poems and his novels also. For a time, I think about pulling out the pages with personal inscriptions. Do I really want someone else to read his inscriptions? I decide anyone can read his personal inscriptions. They can make up a story about me, this Elise who has had loving inscriptions written to her, an Elise who has either died or given away her books with personal inscriptions or they would not have ended up for sale on the street or in a secondhand bookstore. I rip out one poem, dedicated to my initials, from his latest collection. Then I throw out that collection also. I give away the red bracelet he has given me and the violet scarf. I lose the black rose earrings. I ditch a hat he bought me and a pair of Timberland shoes for walking. I toss a lock of his hair I have kept for eight years. I keep a cassette of his voice messages on my answering machine. Never will I answer their call.

48

Alain is from Queens, and in freight. He has six vintage cars, one Jaguar, one Lincoln Navigator SUV and three Ducati motorbikes. He has a house on the Brooklyn Heights Promenade with twenty rooms. The rooms are empty because his wife has just left him. "I hate you," she says, on his answering machine. "I hate you." He is broken, and very gentle. *You have saved me*, he writes, *from the jaws of despair*. He buys me a leather blazer and Frederic Fekkai haircuts. He buys me Cole Hahn shoes and a tank watch from Coach. When he has known me longer, he says, he will buy me a better watch. In the next months he has two hair transplants, an eyelift and a nose job. He buys his own plane so he can pick up his young daughters from their mother's upstate. I watch them run toward us on the tarmac— the pretty one and the one he loves best. Their first night with him, I stay over at his house to help him. They scream at 8:00 p.m. and at 10:00 p.m. and at 4:00 in the morning. I put the youngest in the bed. She is three and falls out, screaming. "Maybe I should leave," I say, thinking I am stressing them. It is New Year's Day, at 6:00 a.m. Alain takes me by the hair and tosses me down the stoop. When we try to reunite, some months later, he apologizes. Once, he admits, he had a man's legs broken. "You need to be tougher," he says. "You need to negotiate." Later, he marries a fashion designer from Russia. She is blonde and wears four-inch heels and I see them online, posing before his Rolls Royce, in matching animal furs.

49

can't we please
make peace? I can't
imagine that you could
be any happier with
the present state of
affairs than I am

Devil

50

Gerardo is from Spain. When he was born, his father named an oil tanker after him. His sister, too, had a tanker named after her: the *Paloma*. Gerardo is wild and has children. I live with him and his male lover and his children in an antebellum house. "Everything is beautiful here," I tell the Mormon men who visit. We have two Great Danes, three doves, two pythons, and a turtle. We have parrots and an Oldsmobile and a white BMW. We drink Martinis. Gerardo makes Spanish omelets. When he thinks his lover is out with someone else, we take the Oldsmobile, at dawn, and smash it into the back of the BMW. We drive to the Delta—long and dry and dark—and Gerardo tosses the lit butt of his cigarette from the car into the field. "You can't do that," I say. "*Oh come, come on,*" he says, "*get over it.*" We play opera and Patsy Cline. We lace cigarettes with cocaine. He pours vodka straight into the glass. "Princess," he warns, when men come by, looking for cocaine, for sex, for me, "this is not the one for you."

51

I meet Hugh at the St. Mark's Bookstore. He is twenty-two and I am thirty-seven and he is reading Bukowski. "You're hot," he says. "You're so hot." He is 6'4". He is an actor and "should try Chekhov," I say. "Your hands are shaking," he says. "Why do your hands shake?" My hands shake, I tell him, because I have been through some things. "What things?" he asks. "What is your number and where do you live?" Outside, on the street, I let him kiss me. *You crazy leaf,* he writes me later. *I want to stop your hands from shaking for good.* When he comes over, he sprays air freshener on his red plastic sneakers. His body is too big for me and that is ok, he says, he is used to it. "You're not disappointed?" I ask. He shrugs. "When did you lose your virginity?" I ask. "When I was twenty-one," he says. That seems quite late to me. Then I realize, that means he was a virgin last year. On the way out, he asks if he can borrow $20. "For weed," he says. He wants to come back later, but I don't let him. He is too young for me, I say. He pauses at that. "I'm getting older," he answers. Later, he sends me messages: *Don't let men treat you with disrespect. There are assholes out there but I'm not one of them.*

52

Joe throws me on the bed. It is a high bed, luxurious, with all white linen. His entire apartment is white, nothing on the walls but a photograph of Jimi Hendrix. "You're rough," I complain. "You seem to like it," he answers. I don't really. He is a successful painter. He paints horses mostly, and sometimes dogs. He is "jaded beyond belief," he tells me. But women love him. He doesn't know why. I don't know why either. It is a mystery.

As usual, I decide to win him over. We lie back on his white sheets, his white duvet, his layers of thick white pillows. His hair is lanky and sweaty and dark. I touch it, with my fingers; I lay it against mine: dark on white. He smiles. Then he brushes my hand away.

"With most women," he tells me, "you have to work to get at their sex side. But with you," he says, "it's all right on the surface." He tells me a story. Once, he had an assistant. She washed his brushes and refreshed his paints. One morning, in his studio, he tripped and caught her hand. They fell into each other, they rolled and collided and ended up having sex. From that morning, they always had sex. But each time they had sex, he had to talk to her afterwards—and he didn't want to talk to her. Then, soon, she started balking at washing his brushes. As if someone else should wash the brushes. As if she was his girl-friend. And he didn't want a girlfriend. He wanted someone to wash the brushes. That is a horrible story, I think. Horrible. It takes me a while to recover. Then, slowly, I say to Joe, "I would wash your brushes."

Part Two

The first day I saw Ben was in Central Park. Yellow flowers pushed their way out of the lush watered grass. I was in Sheep's Meadow with my mother and her boyfriend, Steve Galogly. We had a picnic rug and bags of food from Zabars.

"There he is," Steve said and raised his hand. Ben went to boarding school upstate. He was eight years older than I, and seventeen. He didn't wave back. He just raised his hand, as if to say, *All right, I see you.* He didn't smile, either. He came along the green fence, slowly, and deliberately, across the long grass. He was large and solid, bigger than his father. He hardly looked like a teenager, more like a workman at the edge of the road, repairing something. He was wearing jeans, and a white t-shirt. His head was bent, as if he had just been told off.

We unpacked bagels and lox and tapenade and champagne. Ben sat on the corner of the rug, his knees up, his hands clasped. He had strawberry blonde hair on his arms. It was lighter than the hair on his head, which was a brownish rust color and cut very short. Steve opened the champagne. You were not supposed to drink in the park. But this was a special occasion. My mother's plastic glasses were pale pink, so the champagne looked rose inside them. "Ben," Steve said, "Elise. Your mother has agreed to become my wife." Ben's eyes—amber like a lion's—slid slowly from left to right. I caught my image in the corner of them, me with my blonde plaits under my broad-brimmed sunhat. "A new family," my mother announced.

Ben finished his drink. His fingernails were bitten to the point of bleeding. He took a cigarette from a packet in his jacket and stood up.

"You are not smoking that now," Steve said, "Not in front of your new sister." Ben cast his eyes skyward, then slowly my way.

"Did you ever have a sister?" he asked, misquoting, I now know, William Faulkner. "Well, I did," he said, still misquoting, "And she was a bitch."

He had never had a sister, before me. And never once did it seem to me that I was his sister. He had just been expelled from school. He had been expelled, my mother told me, from every school he had been to. He was expelled in England when he lived with his mother. And he'd been expelled three times since he had come to the States. It was drugs, my mother said, and running away. But mostly, she said, it was "refusal." Refusal to "participate." I didn't know about this. All I knew was he was walking off. "See you," he said.

We moved into Steve Galogly's apartment on upper Fifth Avenue. It was almost a bad neighborhood, at this time. But his apartment was huge: a ten room space that after the renovations became a great open rectangle with small bedrooms facing east. It was on the tenth floor; the elevator had little seats you could pull down.

By the time my mother and I moved in, three months after the Central Park lunch, one month before the wedding, Ben was in a boarding school in North Adams, Massachusetts. Even with his record, Steve always found a new school that would take him. This was because, first, Steve Galogly was a headmaster. He knew all the schools and all the heads of the schools. Second, when Ben took admissions tests, he got the highest scores. When schools saw these scores, they were bowled over. They thought he could be someone, could reflect some light on them. Schools needed that. Schools sought out the gifted like nubby bits of gold—rough and ugly sometimes, but worth something.

Why didn't Ben go to his father's school, I asked my mother, to the school in Riverdale where Steve Galogly was principal? He went there once, my mother answered.

I liked the new apartment. I liked my new room. It was off the kitchen and my mother spent three weekends decorating with me. She wanted me to choose a pink room, a girly room, but I preferred sky blue. Also, I liked silver. In our old house, in Long Island, my mother never decorated my room. Steve had more money, though my mother didn't say this. She said things should be easier for us now, easier for me. I didn't think things had been so hard. But that was because I didn't remember my father, not the way she did. I was three when he died. All I remembered was the smell of his cigarettes and his dark hair that hung over his eyes and sitting on our living room carpet playing Pick-Up Sticks and Barrel of Monkeys. Barrel of Monkeys was my favorite. The barrel was blue and the monkeys red, blue, and green. I still have the barrel. I've lost two of the blue monkeys and the red ones have their arms chewed. That was from me I guess. When we played my father was always very earnest and serious. Too serious, my mother says.

Ben turned seventeen on the 20th of November. Steve called him on the phone, before dinner, from the living room where he was on his second bottle of low carb beer. "Say hello to your brother," my mother said, pushing me toward the phone. I took it from Steve, though I didn't want to. "Happy Birthday Ben."

"I do not love you," he said, this boy I had met only once, "except because I love you." He was quoting Pablo Neruda, though again I did not know this yet. I didn't know what to say and I didn't say anything for the longest time. I heard him breathing down the phone, then start to whistle. It was a casual melodic whistle, a kind of innocent and unaffected tra-la-la. "Well, goodbye," I said.

My father was a high school teacher, of mathematics. He was smarter than that, my mother says, but he had "performance anxiety." When he went on interviews, he broke out in a sweat; his mind became empty of everything but fear. After his last interview at Peter Stuyvesant School, he was hit and killed by a Lincoln Continental in lower Manhattan. My mother and I moved to Montauk to an apartment in another family's house. It had a side entrance and one bedroom. I slept on a cot in the living room that we put out at night. We were so near the ocean we could smell it.

Steve was happy I had spoken to Ben. Steve didn't ask, however, what Ben had said to me. "Elise," he said, my step-father who ran not just a school for children, but teenagers also, a whole gigantic school. "It's good to have you here." The next month, he officially adopted me. They even changed my name. I now had the same last name as Ben. I was Elise McKnight Galogly. The McKnight was for my father, though it was not for a long time that I again used this name.

Of course, I had my friends in Montauk, Lisa and Sharon and Jane, but it was exciting, moving to the city. My mother was excited and Steve Galogly adopted me and I would not go to Mr. Galogly's school, but to a church school, an Episcopal school, my mother called it. But this story was not about school, which you knew by now, if you'd been listening to me—which you might not have been. Only people who really loved you cared about your childhood, and even then, some of them were only being polite.

Ben didn't come to the wedding. He didn't come to Thanksgiving. Maybe he would never come home, I thought. People ran away at his age, didn't they? But then he came for Christmas. He came in the front door with a duffel bag, in a strange woollen jacket they used to call a lumberjacket, and a gray woollen beanie. He hardly spoke to me or my mother. He didn't stay home for dinner. Later at night, he argued with Steve in the kitchen.

When I came home from school he was often in the living room watching television. He didn't want to talk to me. He wanted to be left alone—"And leave him alone," my mother warned me, "he won't be here for long." How wrong was she there? How utterly and completely wrong. I could write it on her gravestone, if it came to that one day: *He won't be here for long.*

He had the room next to mine. It was a smaller room, without windows. Mostly, he kept the door closed. The few times I saw it open, his clothes were spilling out of his duffel bag. His bed was unmade and there were paperbacks on the floor, old secondhand ones such as *A Clockwork Orange* and *Tinker Tailor Soldier Spy.* He had put nothing on the walls.

I tried to speak to him the first week. My mother tried to speak to him. He answered her sometimes, the quickest way he could. He never answered me though. I came into the kitchen where he was standing up, drinking coffee while my mother was at the stove. "Do you like your new school?" I asked him. "Do you miss England?" I asked. "What do you want to do after school?" None of these questions did he answer.

"Please, Benjamin," my mother said, and he just looked at her, as if he didn't understand why he was being addressed, at all. Then they went out one night, my mother and his father. They left me before a movie with a box of chewy fruits. It was the first time I had been alone with Ben in the apartment. Would he come out of his room? I wondered. Would he finally speak to me? I heard him in the kitchen opening a soda. I heard him walking toward me. "Chewy fruits?" he asked, from behind me. I turned to look at him. Was he going to be nice? This time I was the one who didn't answer. Then he came around the couch, and sat opposite me. My feet were bare; I drew them in, away from him. He sat his soda on the coffee table. "Are you going to watch something?" I pointed to the DVDs on the table before us. He smelled of something—or not of something exactly. He smelled warm, as when you've stayed inside a long time. He was wearing his usual house clothes: sweatpants and a sweat-shirt with a hoodie. His feet were bare. They were blocky and slightly pink. "Do you want to talk now?" I asked him.

"I didn't say I want to talk."

"Don't you like it here?"

"No," he said, "I don't like it here."

His eyes were very blue. They were the only part of him that was bright, like dolls' eyes, almost.

"What happened to your real Dad?" he asked me then.

"A car accident."

"That's all you know?"

"A car hit him, in the city."

"That's what they told you?"

I felt a strange burning inside my stomach then, an alarm or warning sign. "Yes."

His face was like his feet: pale but with a pinkish tint. He was almost a redhead, though not quite. Now that he was talking, I finally got to ask him what I really wanted to. "Do you have any other sisters, brothers? In England?"

"No."

"Or cousins or anything?"

"No."

I was disappointed. My mother had said he was an only child, too, but I always wished I had more relatives.

"Why are you sitting like that?" he asked.

"Like what?"

"All scrunched up in the corner."

I unfolded my legs. I was wearing a purple skirt, and a silver t-shirt.

Ben touched my foot. His hand was larger than Steve Galogly's hand, and rougher. Maybe he was adopted, too. "How old are you?" he asked.

He knew how old I was.

"Girls get their periods now at nine. Do you have your period?"

I would not tell him that.

"Have you ever had a boyfriend?"

I had not had a boyfriend. Unless you counted Peter with his dead fly, or Bruce who bought me ice blocks and a bracelet and a Parker pen.

Ben lowered his voice. "Do you want to know how it feels?" I felt my chest expand, as if with air. I was holding my breath. What did he mean?

"How what feels?" I asked, the hair on my head seeming to prickle a little.

"How it feels to have a boyfriend."

Something in my body started to soften then. Something warmed. Something flowed like night. "Close your eyes," he said. I would not close my eyes. "Lie back on the couch." I would not lie back on the couch. "You're scared." I was scared. He moved his hand. He moved it up my skirt and then he touched me, under my underpants. "Are you wet now?" he asked. What did he mean, was I wet? "That's what happens to girls," he said, "when men touch them."

I didn't know if I was wet or not. All I knew was that something had happened in my body, that as much as I wanted to tell him to leave me alone, as much as I wanted to leave and go to my room, I stayed on the couch. His face was very serious, very close. His eyebrows were the color of his hair, reddish brown. "I'll show you," he said. "How it feels. You'll know then."

He had a girlfriend in those days. I didn't know it yet. Her name was Melanie. He had had her for three years. She had been thirteen when they met and he fourteen. He still saw her, though not so much since he'd gone to North Adams. "Everyone does it," Ben said.

I felt the thick edge of his thumb against my skin. A thrill went through me, the kind you get at top speed in a lurching boat, in high wind on a rocky ocean. "Close your eyes," he said. My body was full and warm and soft all at the same time. My body felt heavy and full of something that felt half good and half sort of painful, something I had never felt before. When I closed my eyes, when I lay my head for a minute back on the edge of the couch, he pulled more vigorously at my panties. At the same time, he leaned down and pressed his mouth into me. He sucked at me, long and hard and warm and a terror of softness. I gasped then. I pulled back from him. He slid his fingers between my legs. "You're wet now," he said. His eyes were bright with a glint of light, and at the same time narrowed. His mouth was wet and somehow curled like an accusation. "More?" he asked.

He didn't have to tell me that it was wrong. I knew it was because of the smirk he gave me, the one that made me feel slightly sick. I knew from the way he got up suddenly and wiped his face, went to his room and slammed the door, that we weren't suddenly friends the way I had thought we might be. I felt a great wave of something dark and terrible come over me then, as if I should break something, or even better break myself against something. Why had I let him touch me? At the same time, I had never felt anything like that before. Was this like drugs that my mother said he took? Was this sex, that all the adults kept secret? Part of me wanted, already, for him to come back.

The next days, if anything, were worse than before between us. He still no longer spoke to me, but he spoke about me. "Does she have to come?" he asked when we went out to dinner. "Does she still play with Little Ponies?" he asked while getting orange juice. "Why bother?" he told Steve who was helping me with math. Then one night my mother and Steve were watching a movie in their bedroom. I was in my room trying to sleep, but I had my door ajar and saw Ben go into the kitchen. Then he was at my door. I couldn't see his face, just the shape of him. When he spoke his voice was very soft. "What am I going to do now?" he asked. His voice was so sly, I didn't like him at all. I wanted to sit up and scream. Instead my body went the way it had when he touched me, full of longing. I held my breath. I thought I might cry. "You can say 'Stop it,'" he said. "If you say 'Stop it,' I will stop. If you say anything besides that, I will not stop at all." Then he came to the bed.

And then it went on. That Christmas and during his spring break and during the summer. At his graduation from high school when we stayed in North Adams. On nights he was home and on days after school. Every day I swore I would not let him touch me again. Every day, I failed. He would not have a conversation with me. He only repeated things I said to him:

"Leave me alone. Stay away from me. Don't touch me." He laughed at these words. He sang them over and over. I sobbed in my room. It wasn't he who I hated as much as myself. Because they were just words, and we both knew this. They were just words, and in the end, when the lights were out, and the desire for pleasure came up against my hatred, I always gave in. On the bed, on the couch, on the bathroom floor, I always gave in. I would say "don't," or I would say "no" or I would even say "stop," but I never said "stop it," did I? And both of us knew that.

Then he got into a small college upstate, called Alfred. Steve was sure he'd drop out before he even went. Ben, he said, did everything he could to fail him; it was his revenge, he said, for the fact that Steve had left his mother, for the fact that Steve was a high school principal; what better way to hurt his father, than to fail at school? And of course, what more futile way. Because it only hurt Ben, in the end. I wished Ben would succeed in getting away from Steve. I wished he would disappear. I even wished that he would just die—with his mockery and his scorn, his drugs and his secrecy.

He made it through two years at Alfred, studying French poetry, reading Spanish. I was thirteen when we visited and my parents left me with Ben at his dorm. He closed the door and I closed my eyes and "You'll be old enough soon," he said.
    "For what?" I asked.
    "For fucking."

They never guessed, my mother or Steve Galogly. Not the first night when I slept flushed on the couch, afraid to return to my room, not the next or any other or any place or anywhere. Not in the Florida Keys where we vacationed on a sailing boat, not in Montauk on the ocean or Myrtle Beach where Steve's mother lived. They were so often out. It was so often just Ben and me.

It isn't right, my mother said to Steve, to Ben and to me, that a girl as young as I should hate so much. "I can't stand it with them," my mother said and then they went out again, to movies and to the theatre, to the opera and the ballet and school events. To parties. To openings. They left us to sort it out, to make amends, to come to some understanding. All that happened was I lay in my room, wishing Ben dead. And then would come his soft and winding whistle and I'd face the wall. I'd pretend to sleep. I'd hear him, slipping down the hall, in his jeans and t-shirts, his grubby sweatshirts, his bare thick feet. After his junior year, he disappeared. Someone found his typewriter and it had a sheet of paper in it. On the paper were the words Arthur Cravan. Cravan, it turned out, was born in Lausanne in 1887, a boxer and a surrealist. His aunt was married to Oscar Wilde. He disappeared in 1918 on his way to Buenos Aires to see his wife.

"At least he's told you," my mother told Steve. "That he's disappeared on purpose." But Steve could never give up with Ben. As he had never given up finding him new schools, new chances, using his connections to place him in yet another school that would regret taking him. Steve put a detective on him.

They traced him to Colombia. Steve flew down to try to bring him back. He wouldn't come back though. He was working as a bartender. He had a place on the beach.

Three years later, he called from Puerto Rico. He had been arrested. Despite the lawyers and the wrangling and Steve's trips to Puerto Rico, there was little Steve could do. Ben served four years. For me, this was probably the best time of my life. Time I never had to see him, never had to fear him, time when I knew he would never arrive at home, never show up at my door, never be able to reach me. Then my mother called me into her room. Ben was being extradited. He was coming back home to live. He had had a terrible time. I would not recognize him. I would have to try not to be shocked, not to make him feel worse than he did.

"But he's twenty-five," I told her. "I don't want to live with him."
  "However you feel about him," she started to say.
  "You know how I feel."
  "You have to move on. You have to forgive."
  He did not look the same, it was true. He was heavier. His face was pocked. It was broader and whiter. He had a scar

above his right eyebrow. His mouth was thinner than before and straighter. His hair had gone brownish. That first night, when all was dark, I waited in my room. Would he come in? Would it be the same? My room was dark with a small lamp clasped to my headboard. It was hard for me to breathe. I was waiting, and the fear of my waiting set my hair on end. Then he was standing at the door, his figure heavy and hulking, his eyes dulled and his face unreadable, impenetrable. This was when I screamed, so high and loud that I heard the screams as if they were around me, coming from outside and not from me? Ben stared at me, as if my screams didn't register somehow, so unexpected were they. Then he blinked, his body recoiled, he turned back, suddenly, away and into his room. Steve came, and my mother, who sat on my bed. "You've had a dream," she said, in her nightgown and robe, "did you have a dream?" I nodded. My chest felt shaken, as if I'd been battered somehow. "What was it that scared you?" Steve Galogly asked, going to my window and pulling down the blind.

"Ben," I said, "Ben."

"What happened with Ben?"

Ben came back into the room, listing, twisting his hands, shaking his head. I clutched my mother's hand. My own hands were chilled. "I was at the door," Ben said, softly, so softly. "I must have scared her."

"What did you want?" Steve asked him.

How could I tell them, when half of it was my doing?

"Nothing," he said.

"Elise?"

How could I say? I, who even invited him sometimes, with one of our secret codes, so no one else would know.

Instead, I started to cry. Like the child I was, the weak infant.

"It's been a big day," Steve said.

"I'll bring you some warm milk," my mother said.

He stayed out of my way, after that. He didn't speak to me, or mock me or upbraid me. He simply kept his eyes off of me, and his body. He kept himself away, the way he always should have.

My mother was right that he had been through something. All the threat had gone out of him, all the energy and brio. He was a weight, a kind of laggard.

Finally one day he sat beside me at the kitchen table. I felt my body tense up. I didn't want to be near him. Then he looked up at me, nervously, in case I might scream again, or even do something violent. That was how I felt now, when he was around me. As if I wanted to slice him with a knife, to throw my body into him.

"I'm sorry," he said, "for how I treated you."

"You're sorry?"

"I'm sorry."

"Just like that?" I asked.

"Not just like that. I talked to someone, in prison. I know what I've done."

"You think so?"

"I used you."

It was as if an iceberg fell over a waterfall. I watched it—all our past and our violence. We were left in silence, in a still place. "But I had feelings too, Elise," he went on.

"Other feelings?"

"Yes."

I got up from the table. I backed away toward the door. "I have always hated you." I told him. "I always will hate you."

It was a campaign then, that he began. A long and slow campaign, one I had no awareness of. I was still so young. I didn't know that people planned their relations with others. I didn't think about logistics and goals and wearing down over time.

"How nice," my mother said, that Ben and I had "grown up," that Ben and I were no longer fighting. She knew nothing at all, my mother. She knew not the first thing. Then gradually it eased. The violence in me, the years of it that had gathered together on that one night, slowly settled back into me, repacked itself underneath my skin. He sensed this; he was a tracker. He came up beside me at the kitchen sink. Not behind me where

I might bristle, where I might think he was going to touch me, but to the side of me, carrying an empty plate, crumbs of toast on it. "We are not related," he said. I turned and looked at him, at his dopey amber caramel eyes, medicated with sedatives. I had no answer for him.

He came into the lounge one night. I was sitting alone reading a book. "What do you think I thought about in prison?" I stared at him, at his new dumbness and docility, his calm and his placidity. "You," he said. "You. I thought about you." Maybe that made him feel better, to pretend he cared about me. To pretend there was something between us instead of vileness and sex.

At the same time, it takes effort to carry hatred. When I looked at Ben, suddenly, as a new person, the old terror of a person that lived in me was suddenly negated, suddenly gone. It was such a relief to think that this Ben, this old Ben, was no longer inside me, no longer in the world. How would it be, I began to sense then, if all my hate disappeared like my youth, if after all this time his very hatred of me turned out to be something gentle, turned out to be some kind of caring, some kind of love.

I began once again to be aware of him, to know what room he was in, and if he was silent or murmuring, talking or whistling. I began to sense his body as he walked beside me. I began to think of him again as I lay in bed in the evenings. I watched him week after week, month after month, denuded now, de-wired, a placatory quiet force.

Half of the time, it was just me and Ben in the house. Ben, who acted like he had had ECT. "He has not had ECT," Steve said. Though it was, he admitted, recommended. His medication made him drowsy and complacent. I felt this drowsiness, this heaviness, each time I entered the lounge. That was where he spent his days, reading magazines, writing stories. Around him was a dereliction of plates and glasses and empty Coke cans. He ate shocking food since prison. He ate candy bars and potato chips and fatty pork rinds. Other times he called up for takeout. My mother tried to get him to stop. "It's expensive, and gluttonous." Steve said to let him alone. "He's been deprived so long." Ben ordered fat plates of sushi and hamburgers with bacon and cheese. He ordered thick shakes and plates of ribs with barbeque sauce.

He started going out at 11:00 p.m. and not coming back until early morning. I heard him and Steve beginning to fight about it. It was like the old days . . . Steve "had done everything" he could. I heard his slightly reedy voice rising from the kitchen. "This is not a hotel. This is not a rest stop." I could just imagine the way Ben looked at Steve during these sessions. Not with boredom, exactly, just a certain emptiness. "Don't you want anything?" Steve asked him.

"What do you do all night?" I finally asked him. *The Late Show* was on and Ben was fidgeting to leave.

"Walk around," he said, "Check out neighborhoods."

"Do you go with anyone?"

"Do you want to come?"

"Do I?" I asked him, thinking I had misheard him.

"It would be better if you came."

I admired his stubbornness, the way he refused to give Steve what he wanted.

"I'll look after you," he told me.

"All right," I finally said.

I went to my room and changed. In the street, it was balmy and warm. A tousled cloud of breeze rolled like tumbleweed past us. He kept always to my right, the way men on dates were meant to, protecting me from the street. "Are these friends from school that you see?"

He had one friend, Mark, from North Adams. He had Allan, from the year he was at Fieldston in the Bronx.

We took a cab to the seventies, on the east side. We stepped into a long blue tunnel of a bar, chandeliers like icicles. I was too young to drink so I had sparkling water. The bartender set out olives.

"Do you ever wonder about your Dad?" Ben asked. It had been a long time since I thought about my Dad.

"About what?" I asked.

"Why he killed himself."

He was looking me in the face. There were many years when we never looked each other in the face, when I felt that if I looked at him, something carefully frozen in me would crack into pieces.

"He didn't kill himself." I said.

"You don't think?"

"He was hit by a car."

"Or he was in the path of a car."

"Accidents happen all the time."

He shrugged. "So does suicide."

"Why would he have done that?"

"Failure."

"He wasn't a failure—you don't know how he felt."

"No," he said. "I'm sorry," he said.

"You should be."

He took hold of my wrist. "You're right," he said. "I have no idea. That was mean."

"They say," I announced, swallowing a lime green olive, "that to make up for something really bad you've got to start doing good things, just small good things."

"That's what I'm trying with you."

I remembered the day we met, his eyes like the eyes of a lion, his great thick body like a forester's body, a builder's.

"I told you before," he said. "You're the only one I think of."

"But I hated you."

"You should have."

I looked down at his fingers, his thick rough fingers that had touched me so many times. He placed his hand on my back. His hand was so large and his touch so delicate. It was as if I were glass or something even softer, thin slivers of ice and his warm hand might make me disappear. "Just try to stop thinking of me that way," he said.

"What way?"

"The way you did when you were a kid."

He moved his hand to my face suddenly. His eyes were so close to mine. Never, not since I was nine, had he looked at me so closely. "Elise," he said. The sides of his mouth turned down. He looked for a moment as if might start to cry. It was the first time I had a moment of pity for him. His mouth fell again, deeper, as if he was much older than he was, as if I was seeing him as he'd be in fifty years.

"Nah," he said, and shook his head.

"What?"

"It won't happen."

"What?"

"You," he said, "you," motioning the bartender for another drink. "You won't forgive me."

It felt better to forgive him. I hardly wanted him to know, that it could be so easy for me, just to let him off the hook. I wouldn't have to carry him then. In the street, on the way home, night was burning at the edges, the way paper burned in fire. He took my hand as we crossed the street. He kept it clasped as we moved uptown. I thought for a moment of pulling back. But it was so quiet, in that moment. It was so quiet inside of me.

When you've done something for as long as we had, it was hard to make a change. It was only a matter of time before he loitered at my door. The only difference now was that he looked at me: straight in the eyes, directly. When he did come in, finally, it was dawn. I woke and he was standing at my door, a light jacket in his hand, a packet of cigarettes in his sleeve pocket. He stepped inside and closed the door. He sank into me as if into life. He took off his shirt. He laid his chest against me.

Never would I have believed that I could have forgiven him. Never never never, I used to tell myself. Never let him touch you again. Never speak to him again. All the energy I spent hating him. A great force that for years had run my life.

In August, Steve rented a small summer house in Montauk. My mother and he entertained at night: I saw them the way you see people in a movie, people you don't actually converse with, people in the background of your life. Ben and I went down to the beach, lying salty and damp on our towels.

Where once they could not get us together, where once we had wanted nothing to do with each other, now they could hardly separate us. Now we were hardly ever apart.

In the house, our bedrooms were nowhere near each other. His was at the top, in a small attic. Mine was on the ground floor. I chose it because it had a window onto the side lawn. My mother was showing the rooms to Ben and me and I noticed that he saw it also, this window, that it struck him the way it struck me, as something for us. After that night, all night, I kept the window open. He came in when the moon was perpendicular to the orange tree, below the top windowpane.

Before, I had had no real part in what we did together. It had always been him touching me. Now I lay on my back and looked straight at him. Now he lay on his back with a hand resting on my thigh. We didn't close our eyes. It was a great long drawn-out and slow reverse. It was an undoing. When he groaned, when he said my name, when he uttered any sound, it was as if the silence of the years were suddenly filled, as if we were free for the first time from our own secrecy. It wasn't just sex. It was me as a person he was responding to. It was my body he needed. It was me who he held in the dark and who he watched during the day.

"We should go away," he said, "to California, to the Virgin Islands, to New Mexico. We are not related."

"Should we tell them then?"

He took a breath. He stared at the ceiling. "We don't need to tell them. Not yet."

"But we could."

"He'd kill me if he knew."

I knew in my body when it was pregnant. I knew from my breasts which swelled slightly, and ached. I knew from the taste of Ben in my mouth. Ben was afraid of Steve, and afraid because I was young. I was afraid of everything. We went away for the weekend, to a small hotel where no one could see us. I opened the glass sliding doors and stepped from the porch to the white sand. Being pregnant filled me with longing, to touch Ben and to have him touch me, deeply and completely. I liked the salt on his shoulders when he came in from the sea, the cool of his thighs when he had swum in the ocean, the heat in his hair when he had been in the sun, the odd scattering of sand on his neck or his eyelid.

We didn't know what to do about the baby. "We have to go away," I said. "Or we have to tell them." He didn't answer. I had waves of fear like waves of sickness. Then Ben had a call from an old friend in Colombia. Ben could go ahead, he told me, and "set things up." I knew the minute he said this that he was leaving me. I knew perhaps before he did that he was lying to himself and me. "I'll find a place," he said. "I'll get a job." I was almost three months pregnant. "It's nothing yet," Ben said, tracing lines on my belly, wishing this were the case, for the first time terrified of his father, of what we had done. "It's nothing," he said. "Not yet."

The day he left began at dawn. I stood up and walked out to the kitchen. I went upstairs, quietly, past my parents' room. I went to the attic where Ben never slept. He had rifled through his books. They had fallen awry on the shelves. He had taken his pens and his notebook and his clothes.

He left me an envelope with $500 cash in it. We had lots of time, his note said. I was so young. He couldn't do this to me. I should go to a clinic and later he would come for me.

I did not hear from him. Steve did not hear from him. Steve said, "He's on his own this time, and good luck to him." Each night in the dark I thought I would wait one more day. If I didn't hear from him the next day, I would abort the baby. "How long do I have?" I asked the doctor. "How long? How long?"

"You can do it now," the doctor said, "You can do it now," and then, "You must do it soon." I heard nothing from Ben and nothing again and each day the nothing became a new seed of hate inside me. Each day became the baby that I hated because it was him. It was cursed, it was wrong. It was everything Ben had always been to me. Some kind of hysteria rose in me, a grinding to something unmovable and finite. I thought sometimes that the very rage in me would kill it, that the poison of me would choke it.

Finally, I made the appointment. I wanted nothing now to do with forgiveness, nothing to do with a child neither of us could love. It was Ben and me: corrupt and wrong. A letter came from him next spring. *When are you coming?* Ben wrote. He included a story, "Tumbrel," which I threw away. Later, when I changed my mind and looked up the word, I saw it was a cart used to carry prisoners to the guillotine during the French Revolution.

Appendix
Sergio

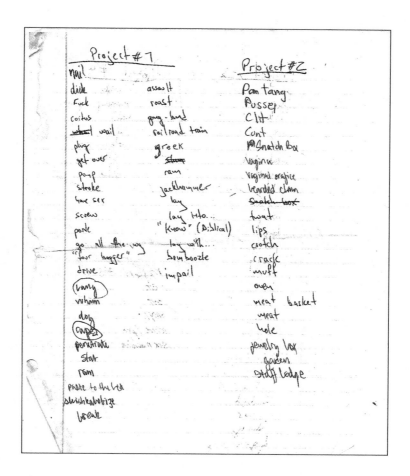

Project #1

nail
dick
Fuck
coitus
~~what~~ wail
plug
get over
pomp
stroke
have sex
screw
pork
go all the way
"four bagger"
drive
bang/whomm
doly
~~come~~
penetrate
stab
ram
paste to the bed
slushkabobize
break

assault
roast
gang-bang
rail road train
greek
~~slut~~
ram
jackhammer
lay
lay into...
"know" (Biblical)
lay with...
bamboozle
impail

Project #2

Pan tang
Pussey
Clit
Cunt
~~M~~ Snatch Box
Vagina
Vaginal orifice
bearded clam
~~Snatch box~~
twat
lips
crotch
crack
muff
oven
meat basket
meat
hole
jewelry box
garden
stuff lodge

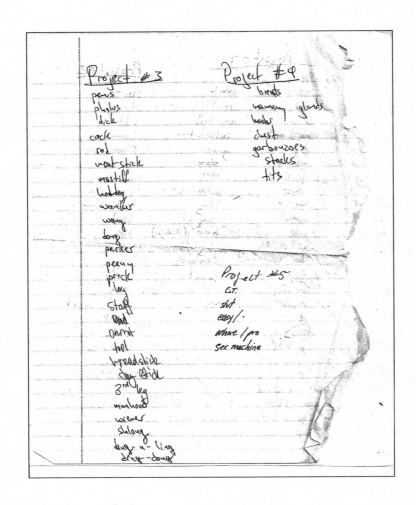

Project #3

penis
phalus
dick
cock
rod
meat stick
mastiff
hotdog
wanker
wang
dong
pecker
peeny
prick
log
staff
maod
carrot
tool
breadstick
joy stick
3rd leg
manhood
wiener
shlong
ding-a-ling
ding-dong

Project #4

breasts
mammery glands
hooter
chest
garbonzoes
stacks
tits

Project #5

C.T.
slut
easy/.
whore / pro
sex machine